HEALTHY LIVING

"Prevent Disease & Live a Healthy Life"

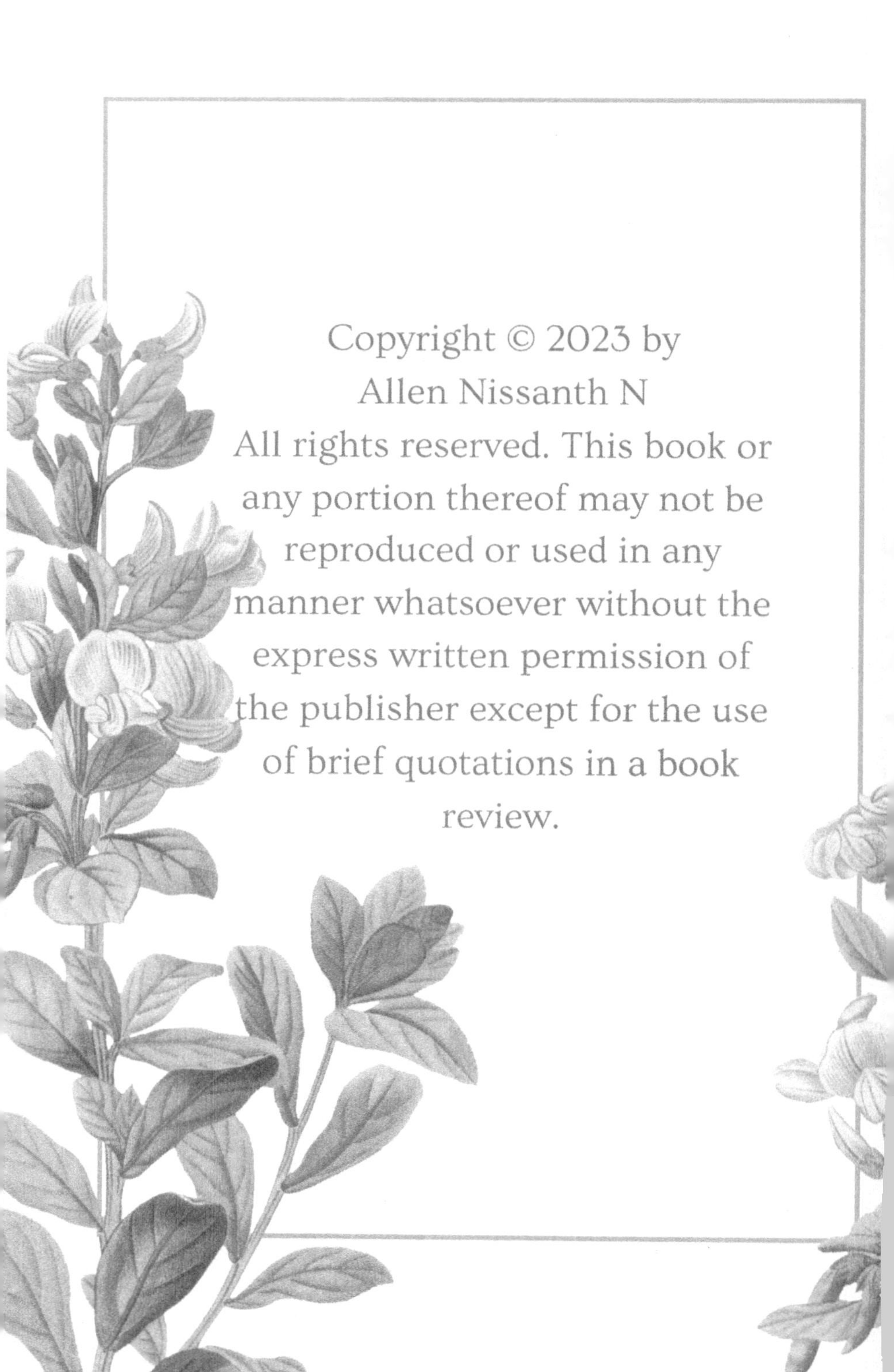

TABLE OF CONTENTS

01. INTRODUCTION

02. HEALTHY DIET

03. REGULAR EXERCISE

04. ADEQUATE SLEEP

05. STRESS MANAGEMENT

06. REGULAR CHECK-UPS

07. HEALTHY WEIGHT

08. AVOID HARMFUL HABITS

07. HYGIENE AND SANITATION

08. GENETIC PREDISPOSITION

09. COMMUNITY AND SOCIAL CONNECTIONS

10. ENVIRONMENTAL FACTORS

INTRODUCTION

Healthy living is a lifestyle choice that prioritizes physical, mental, and emotional well-being. It involves making conscious decisions and adopting habits that promote overall health and vitality. Healthy living encompasses various aspects of life, including nutrition, physical activity, mental wellness, and social connections. It is a journey towards achieving and maintaining a state of optimal health and quality of life.

HEALTHY DIET

FRUITS AND VEGETABLES

Aim to fill half your plate with a variety of colorful fruits and vegetables. They are rich in vitamins, minerals, antioxidants, and fiber, which can help reduce the risk of heart disease, cancer, and other chronic conditions.

WHOLE GRAINS

Choose whole grains over refined grains. Whole grains like brown rice, whole wheat pasta, quinoa, and oats provide essential nutrients and fiber, which can lower the risk of heart disease and diabetes.

LEAN PROTEIN

Incorporate lean protein sources into your diet, such as skinless poultry, fish, beans, lentils, tofu, and lean cuts of meat. These proteins are essential for muscle health and repair.

HEALTHY FATS

Opt for healthy fats like olive oil, avocado, nuts, and seeds. These fats are rich in monounsaturated and polyunsaturated fats, which can support heart health.

DAIRY OR DAIRY ALTERNATIVES

Choose low-fat or fat-free dairy products or dairy alternatives like almond milk, soy milk, or oat milk. These provide calcium and vitamin D for bone health.

LIMIT PROCESSED FOODS

Minimize your consumption of processed foods, including sugary snacks, fast food, and highly processed packaged meals. They often contain unhealthy trans fats, excessive salt, and added sugars, which can increase the risk of heart disease, obesity, and diabetes.

REDUCE SUGAR AND SUGARY DRINKS

Limit added sugars in your diet, such as those found in sugary beverages, candies, and desserts. Excess sugar intake is associated with obesity and an increased risk of type 2 diabetes.

WATCH PORTION SIZES

Pay attention to portion control to avoid overeating. Even healthy foods can contribute to weight gain if consumed in excessive amounts.

STAY HYDRATED

Drink plenty of water throughout the day to stay hydrated. Limit sugary drinks and excessive caffeine intake.

MODERATE ALCOHOL CONSUMPTION

If you consume alcohol, do so in moderation. For most adults, this means up to one drink per day for women and up to two drinks per day for men.

LIMIT SODIUM

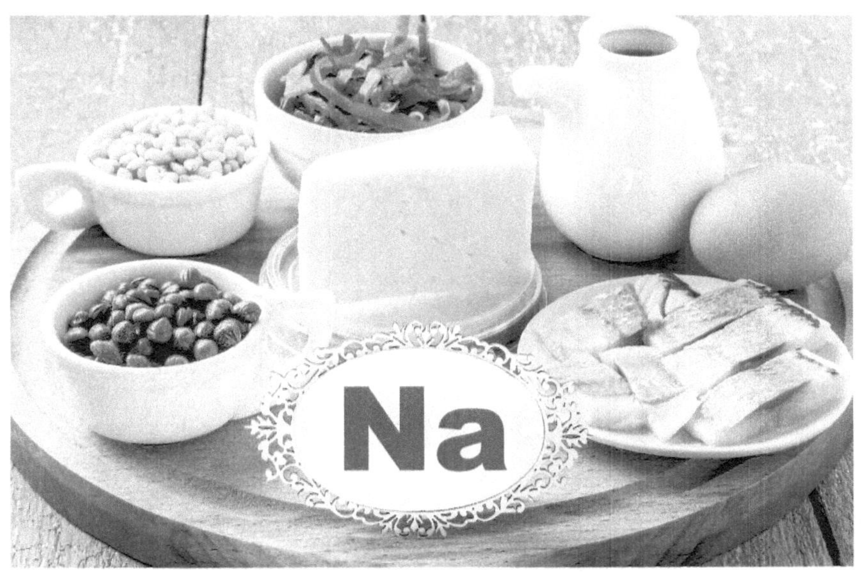

Reduce your sodium intake by minimizing the use of table salt and avoiding high-sodium processed foods. High sodium intake can contribute to high blood pressure and heart disease.

BALANCED DIET

Aim for a well-balanced diet that includes a variety of foods from all food groups. This will help ensure that you get a wide range of nutrients necessary for good health.

CUSTOMIZATION

Keep in mind that individual dietary needs may vary based on factors such as age, gender, activity level, and specific health concerns. It's advisable to consult with a healthcare provider or registered dietitian for personalized guidance.

REGULAR EXERCISE

Improved Cardiovascular Health

Exercise strengthens the heart and improves circulation, reducing the risk of heart disease, high blood pressure, and stroke.

Weight Management

Regular physical activity helps control body weight by burning calories and building lean muscle mass. It can help prevent obesity and related health issues.

Enhanced Muscle and Bone Health

Exercise promotes muscle strength and endurance, which is essential for daily activities and overall mobility. Weight-bearing exercises also help maintain bone density, reducing the risk of osteoporosis.

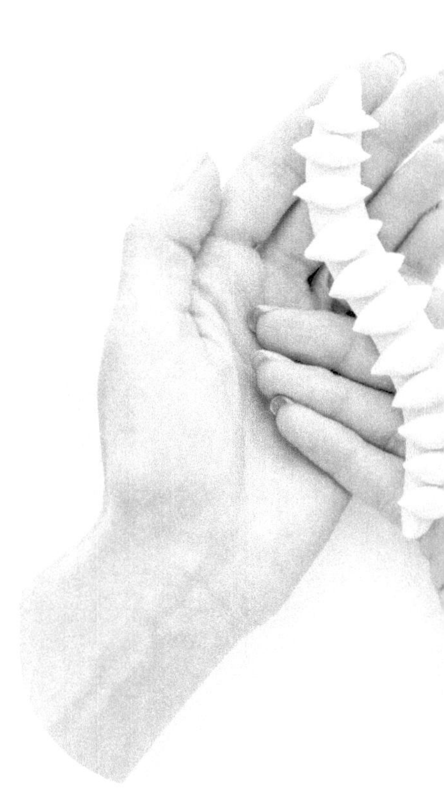

Better Mental Health

Exercise releases endorphins, which are natural mood lifters. Regular physical activity can help reduce symptoms of anxiety and depression, improve sleep, and boost self-esteem.

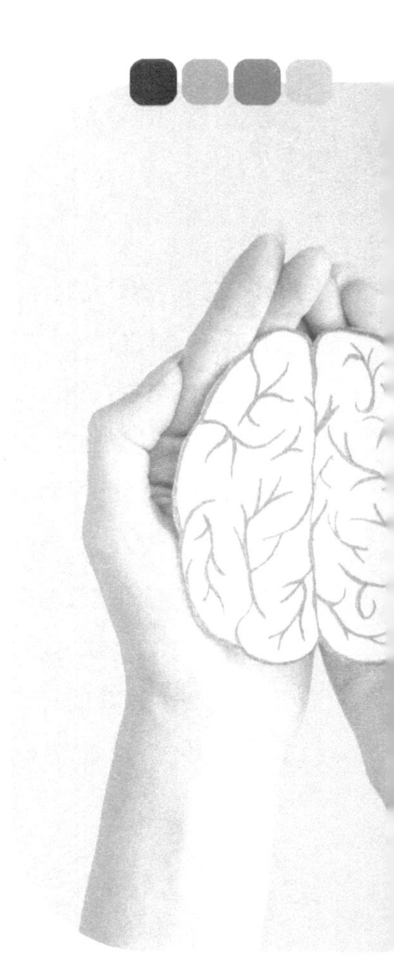

Increased Energy Levels

Engaging in physical activity increases your energy levels and stamina, making daily tasks easier to accomplish.

Improved Metabolic Health

Exercise can help regulate blood sugar levels, reducing the risk of type 2 diabetes and metabolic syndrome.

Enhanced Flexibility and Balance

Certain types of exercise, such as yoga and tai chi, improve flexibility and balance, reducing the risk of falls and injuries, especially as you age.

Reduced Risk of Chronic Diseases

Regular exercise can lower the risk of various chronic conditions, including certain cancers, osteoarthritis, and chronic obstructive pulmonary disease (COPD).

Enhanced Cognitive Function

Physical activity has been linked to better cognitive function and a reduced risk of cognitive decline as you age.

Stress Reduction

Exercise can be an excellent stress reliever, helping you better cope with the demands of daily life.

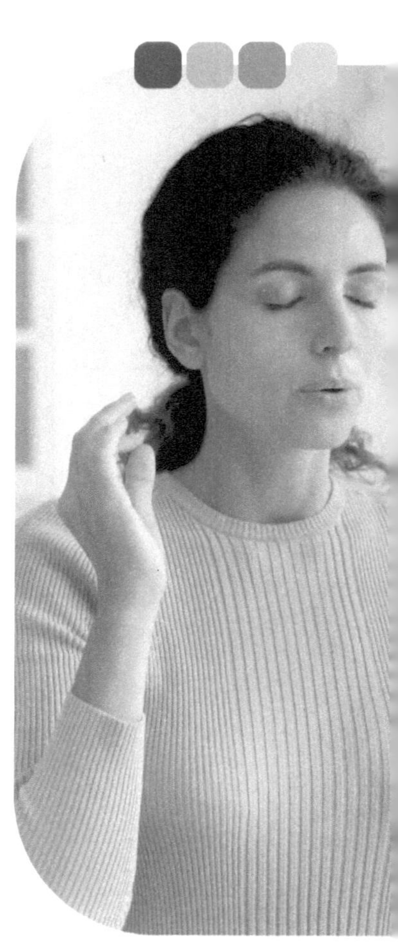

# Social Engagement

Participating in group sports or fitness classes can provide opportunities for social interaction, promoting mental and emotional well-being.

Longevity

Numerous studies suggest that regular exercise is associated with a longer lifespan and a higher quality of life in older age.

ADEQUATE SLEEP

PHYSICAL HEALTH

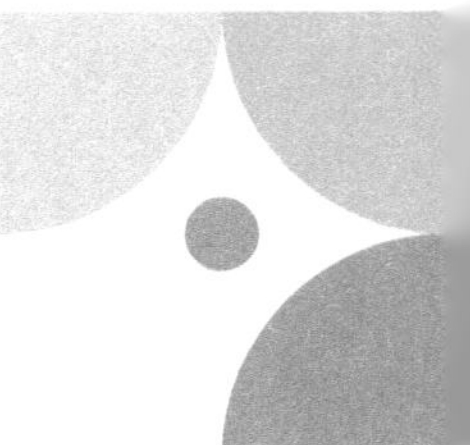

IMMUNE SYSTEM
Sleep helps support a healthy immune system, making it easier for your body to fight off infections and illnesses.

HEART HEALTH
Chronic sleep deprivation has been linked to an increased risk of heart disease, high blood pressure, and stroke.

WEIGHT MANAGEMENT
Lack of sleep can disrupt hormones that regulate appetite, potentially leading to weight gain and obesity.

HORMONAL BALANCE
Sleep is essential for regulating hormones, including those that control growth, stress response, and metabolism.

MENTAL AND COGNITIVE HEALTH

IMPROVED CONCENTRATION
Quality sleep enhances cognitive functions such as concentration, problem-solving, and decision-making.

EMOTIONAL WELL-BEING
Adequate sleep is essential for emotional regulation and mental resilience. Lack of sleep can contribute to mood swings, irritability, and increased stress.

MEMORY CONSOLIDATION
Sleep is crucial for consolidating memories and promoting learning.

PHYSICAL PERFORMANCE

ATHLETIC PERFORMANCE
Athletes often see improvements in performance, coordination, and reaction time with sufficient sleep.

RECOVERY
Sleep is a crucial time for the body to repair and recover from physical activity and injuries.

SAFETY

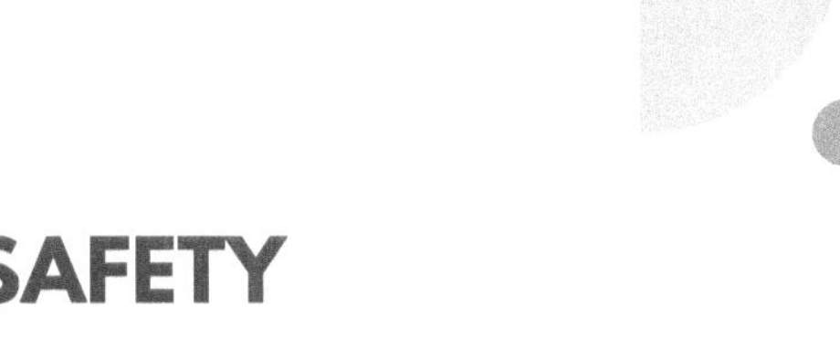

REDUCED ACCIDENT RISK
Fatigue from lack of sleep can impair judgment and reaction time, increasing the risk of accidents, especially when driving or operating machinery.

CHILDREN AND ADOLESCENTS
Adequate sleep is essential for the growth and development of children and teenagers. It supports physical growth, cognitive development, and emotional well-being.

SLEEP TIMINGS

Most adults require 7-9 hours of sleep per night for optimal health and functioning.

Adolescents typically need 8-10 hours of sleep each night.

Younger children may need even more sleep, with recommended ranges varying by age.

PRACTICE MINDFULNESS AND MEDITATION

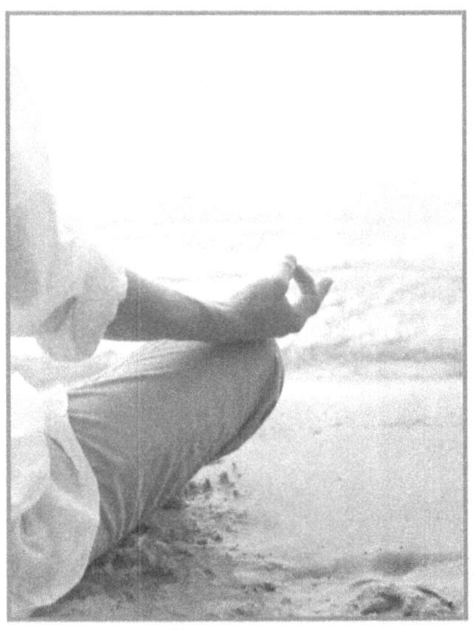

Mindfulness and meditation techniques can help you stay in the present moment, reduce racing thoughts, and alleviate anxiety.

Consider guided meditation apps or classes to get started.

PHYSICAL ACTIVITY

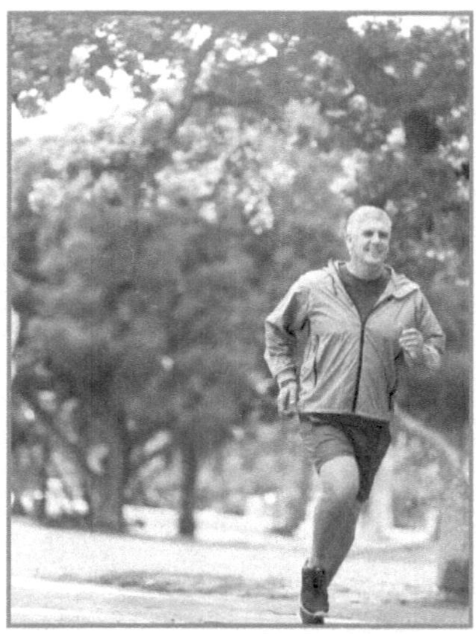

Regular exercise releases endorphins, which are natural mood lifters and stress reducers.

Find physical activities you enjoy, whether it's jogging, yoga, dancing, or walking.

HEALTHY DIET

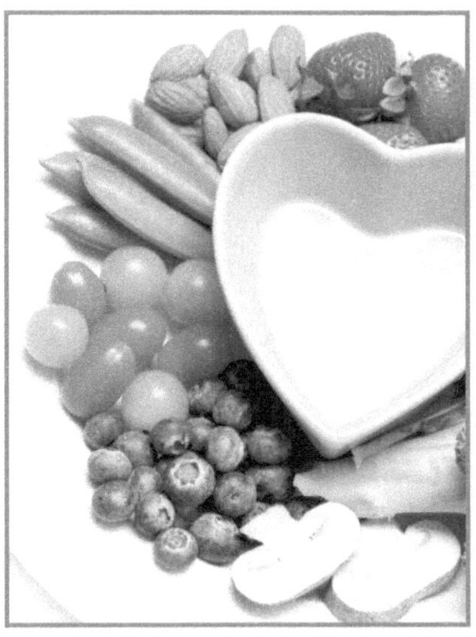

Eating a balanced diet with nutritious foods can help your body better cope with stress.

Avoid excessive caffeine, sugar, and alcohol, as they can exacerbate stress.

ADEQUATE SLEEP

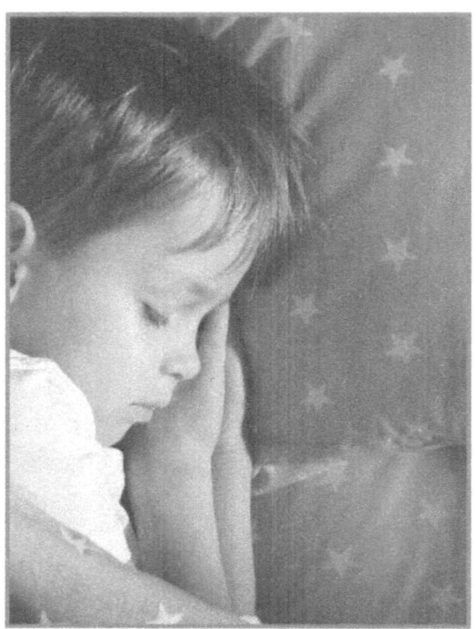

Prioritize good sleep hygiene to ensure you get enough rest. Lack of sleep can make stress feel more overwhelming.

TIME MANAGEMENT

Create a schedule that allows you to manage your tasks and responsibilities effectively. Prioritize and break tasks into manageable steps.

Learn to say no when you have too much on your plate.

DEEP BREATHING AND RELAXATION TECHNIQUES

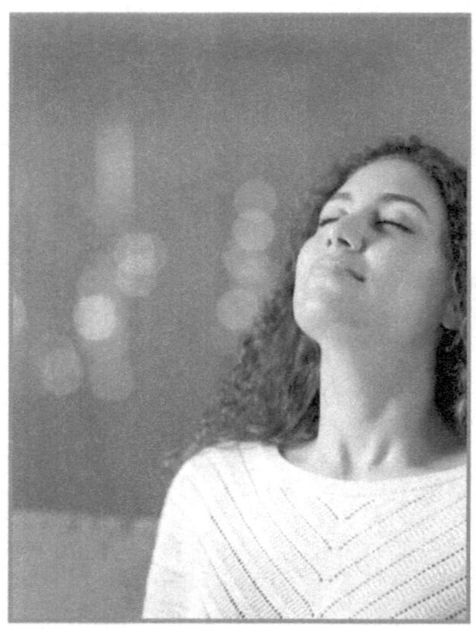

Deep breathing exercises can help calm your nervous system. Practice deep, diaphragmatic breathing when you feel stressed.

Progressive muscle relaxation and visualization techniques can also be helpful.

CONNECT WITH OTHERS

Social support is crucial. Talk to friends, family members, or a therapist about your stressors and feelings.

Spend quality time with loved ones to foster positive relationships.

SET REALISTIC GOALS

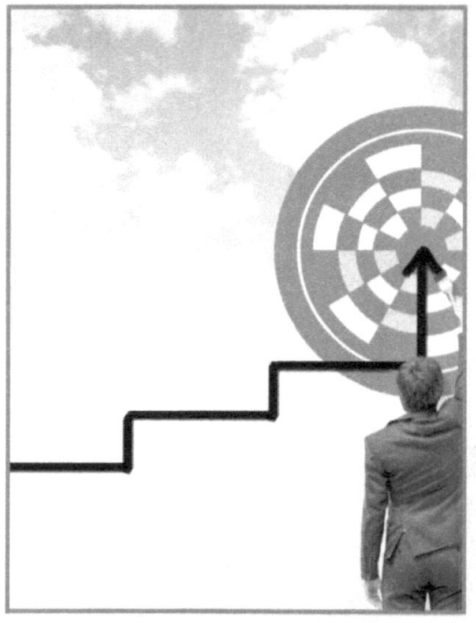

Avoid setting overly ambitious goals that may cause unnecessary stress. Set achievable, incremental goals instead.

HOBBIES AND LEISURE ACTIVITIES

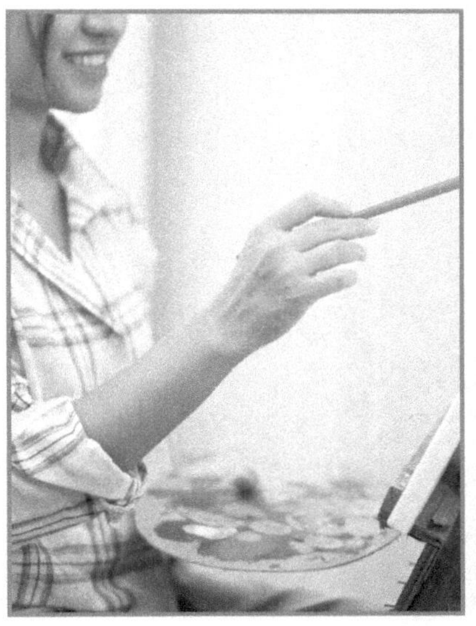

Engage in activities you enjoy to relax and take your mind off stress. Whether it's reading, painting, gardening, or playing a musical instrument, hobbies can be therapeutic.

LIMIT EXPOSURE TO STRESSFUL ENVIRONMENTS

When possible, minimize exposure to environments or situations that consistently cause stress. This may involve making changes in your job, relationships, or daily routines.

PRACTICE GRATITUDE

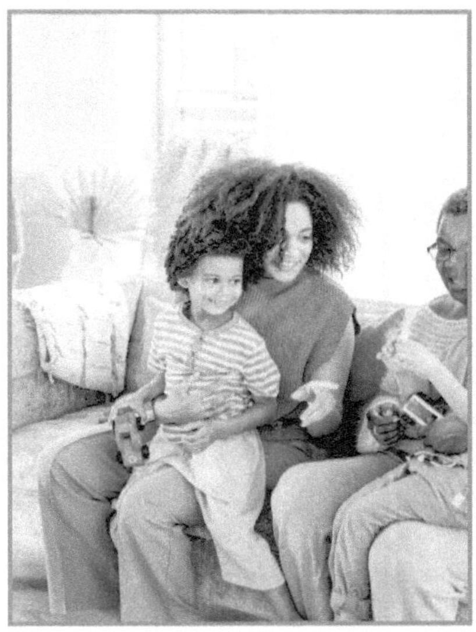

Focus on the positive aspects of your life and express gratitude for them. Keeping a gratitude journal can help shift your perspective.

SEEK PROFESSIONAL HELP

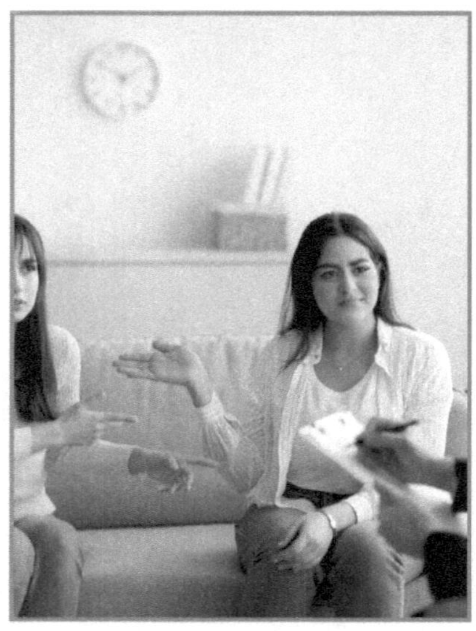

If stress becomes overwhelming and persistent, consider seeking help from a mental health professional, such as a therapist or counselor. They can provide strategies and support tailored to your specific needs.

LIMIT INFORMATION OVERLOAD

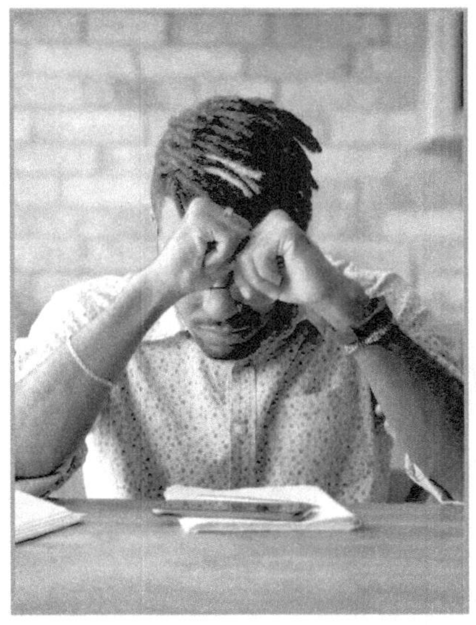

In today's digital age, constant exposure to news and information can be overwhelming. Limit your screen time and choose reliable sources for news updates.

LEARN TO LET GO

Recognize that you cannot control everything. Practice acceptance and learn to let go of things beyond your control.

REGULAR CHECK-UPS

PRIMARY CARE PHYSICIAN

Establish a relationship with a primary care physician or healthcare provider who can serve as your central point of contact for medical care. They can coordinate your healthcare, conduct routine check-ups, and address your general health concerns.

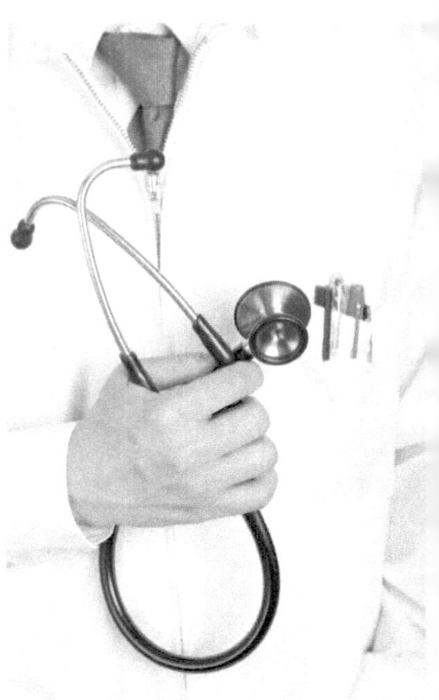

FREQUENCY

The frequency of check-ups may vary depending on your age, gender, medical history, and risk factors. Generally, adults should have a wellness check-up at least annually.

HEALTH HISTORY REVIEW

During check-ups, your healthcare provider will review your medical history, including any chronic conditions, medications, and family medical history.

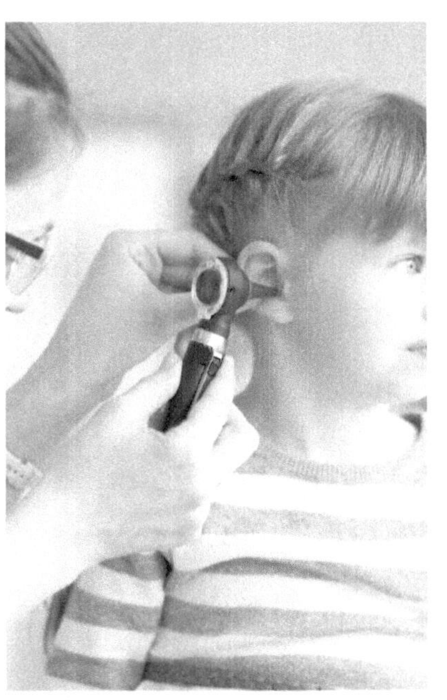

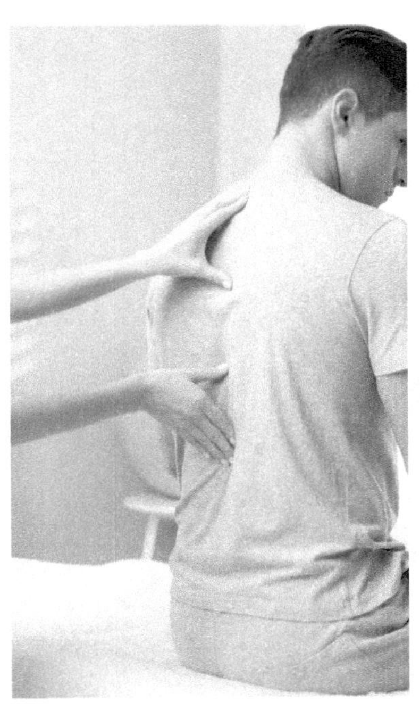

PHYSICAL EXAMINATION

A physical examination is typically part of every check-up. Your healthcare provider will check vital signs (blood pressure, heart rate, etc.) and examine various body systems to assess your overall health.

HEALTH SCREENINGS

Depending on your age, gender, and risk factors, your healthcare provider may recommend specific health screenings such as cholesterol levels, blood glucose, mammograms, colonoscopies, bone density tests, and more.

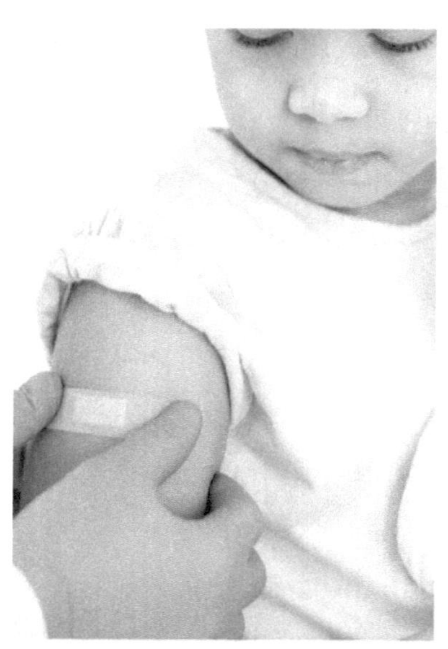

IMMUNIZATIONS

Ensure that your vaccinations are up to date. Vaccines are essential for preventing various diseases.

COUNSELING AND EDUCATION

Your healthcare provider can offer guidance on lifestyle factors such as diet, exercise, stress management, and tobacco/alcohol use. They can also provide information on age-appropriate health concerns and preventive measures.

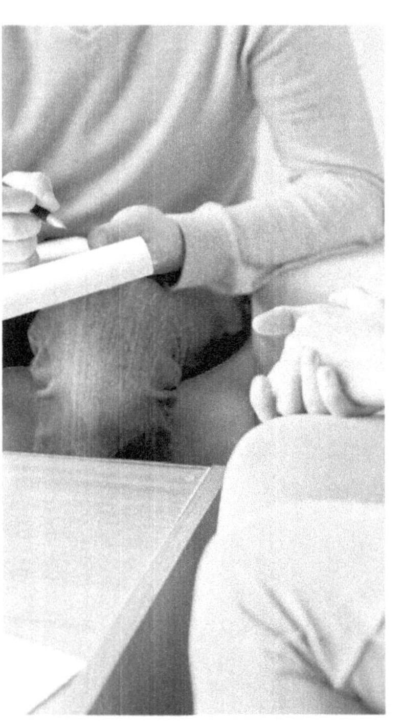

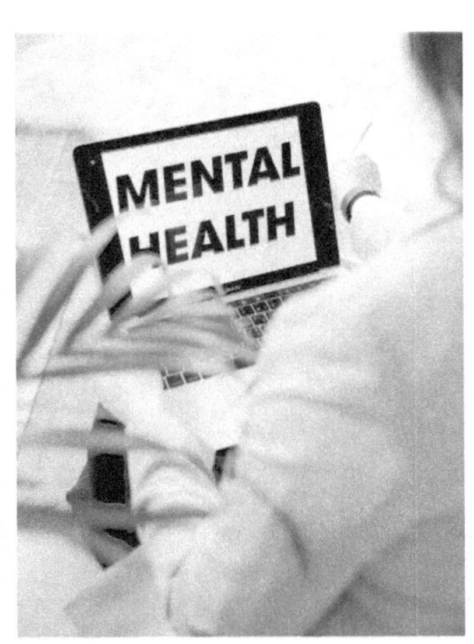

MENTAL HEALTH

Discuss your mental health with your healthcare provider. Mental health is an integral part of overall well-being, and they can provide resources and referrals if needed.

REVIEW MEDICATIONS

If you are taking medications, review them with your healthcare provider. They can check for any potential interactions or side effects.

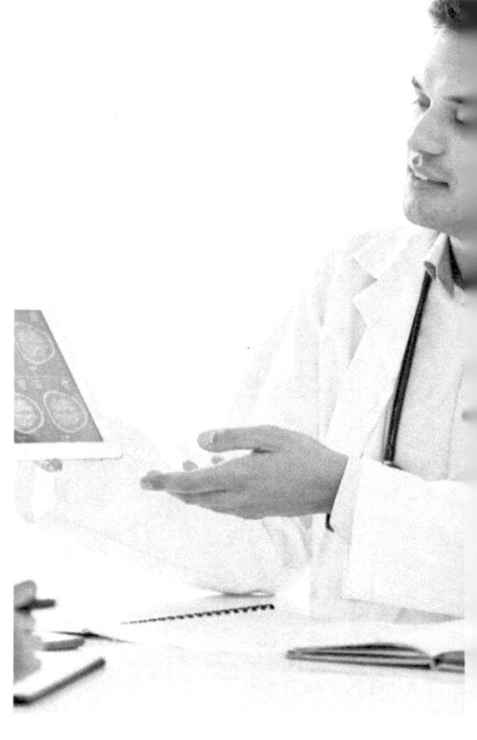

PREVENTIVE CARE

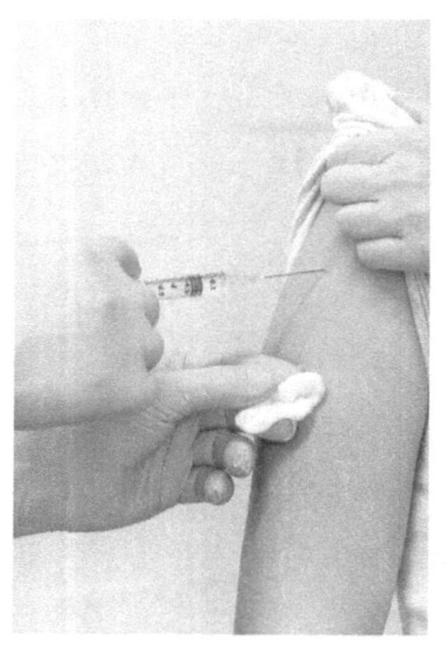

In addition to regular check-ups, preventive care measures like cancer screenings, flu shots, and dental and eye exams should be part of your healthcare routine.

HEALTH GOALS

Discuss your health goals and concerns with your healthcare provider. They can help you set realistic goals and provide support in achieving them.

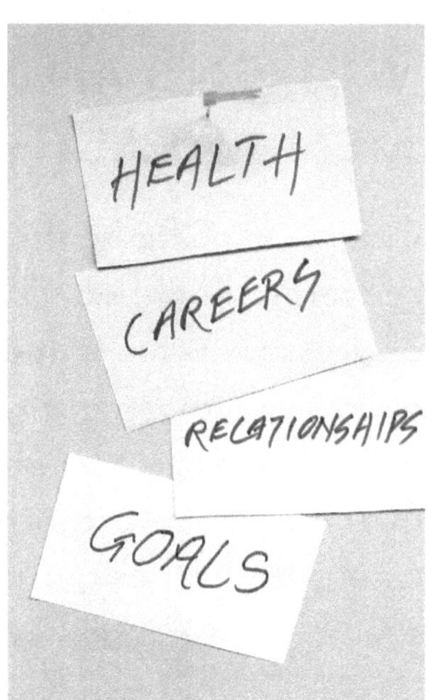

AGE-SPECIFIC CHECK-UPS

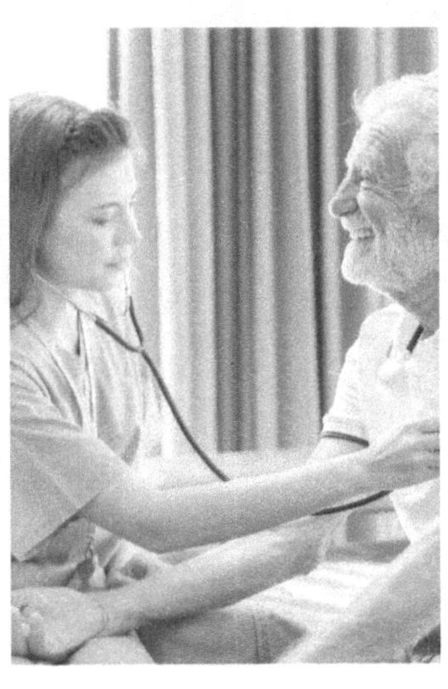

As you age, certain health considerations become more important. For example, older adults may need more frequent check-ups and additional screenings for conditions like osteoporosis or cognitive health.

WOMEN'S AND MEN'S HEALTH

Gender-specific health concerns should also be addressed. Women may need gynecological exams and mammograms, while men may need prostate exams and other gender-specific screenings.

DENTAL AND VISION CARE

Don't forget about your oral and eye health. Regular dental check-ups and eye exams are crucial for maintaining overall health.

HEALTHY WEIGHT

BALANCED DIET

CALORIC BALANCE

To maintain a healthy weight, the number of calories you consume should roughly match the number of calories you burn through daily activities and exercise.

NUTRIENT-RICH FOODS

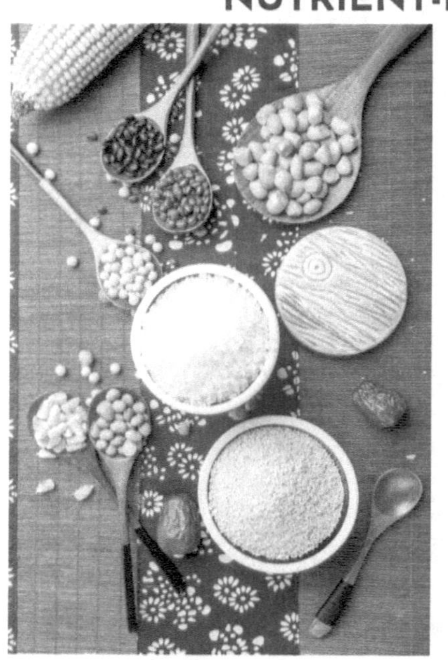

Focus on a diet rich in whole, unprocessed foods, including fruits, vegetables, lean proteins, whole grains, and healthy fats.

BALANCED DIET

PORTION CONTROL

Be mindful of portion sizes to avoid overeating. Use smaller plates and pay attention to hunger and fullness cues.

LIMIT SUGARY AND PROCESSED FOODS

Minimize your intake of sugary beverages, snacks, and highly processed foods, which can contribute to weight gain.

REGULAR PHYSICAL ACTIVITY

- Aim for at least 150 minutes of moderate-intensity aerobic exercise or 75 minutes of vigorous-intensity aerobic exercise per week, as recommended by the American Heart Association.
- Incorporate both cardiovascular (aerobic) exercise and strength training into your routine for a well-rounded fitness plan.
- Find physical activities you enjoy to make exercise a sustainable part of your lifestyle.

LIFESTYLE CHOICES

- Get adequate sleep, as lack of sleep can disrupt hormones that regulate appetite and lead to weight gain.
- Manage stress through techniques like meditation, deep breathing, and relaxation exercises, as stress can trigger emotional eating.
- Avoid excessive alcohol consumption, as it can contribute to weight gain due to its caloric content and impact on inhibitions.

HYDRATION

Drink plenty of water throughout the day. Sometimes, thirst can be mistaken for hunger.

BEHAVIORAL CHANGES

- Practice mindful eating, which involves paying attention to what and how you eat, savoring your food, and eating without distractions.
- Keep a food diary to track your eating habits and identify areas for improvement.
- Set realistic, achievable goals for weight management, and celebrate your successes along the way.

SEEK PROFESSIONAL GUIDANCE

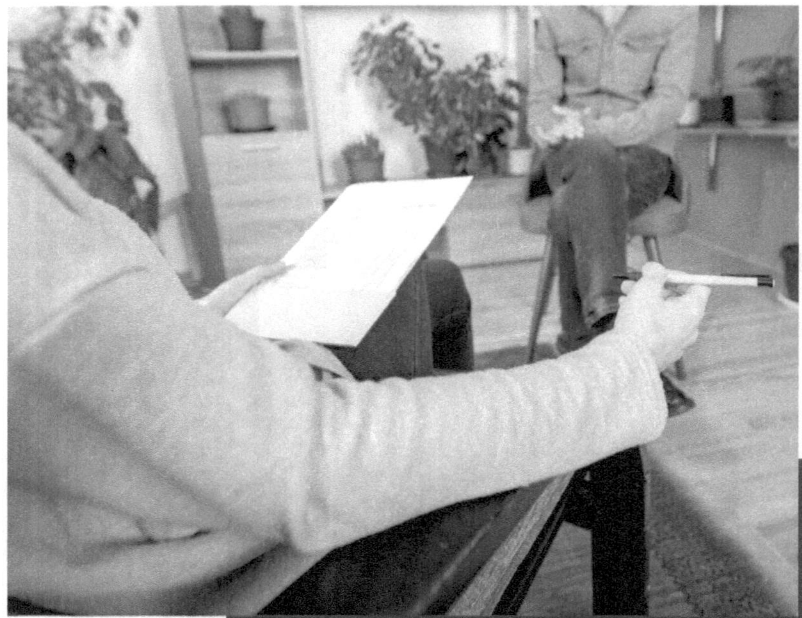

- Consult with a registered dietitian or nutritionist for personalized dietary guidance and meal planning.
- Consider working with a fitness trainer or exercise specialist to create an effective workout plan.

AVOID FAT DIETS

Be cautious of extreme diets that promise rapid weight loss, as they are often unsustainable and can be harmful to your health.

AVOID HARMFUL HABITS

SMOKING AND TOBACCO USE

- Smoking is a leading cause of preventable death worldwide. Quitting smoking is one of the best things you can do for your health.
- Seek support from healthcare professionals, smoking cessation programs, or support groups.
- Consider nicotine replacement therapy or prescription medications to aid in quitting.

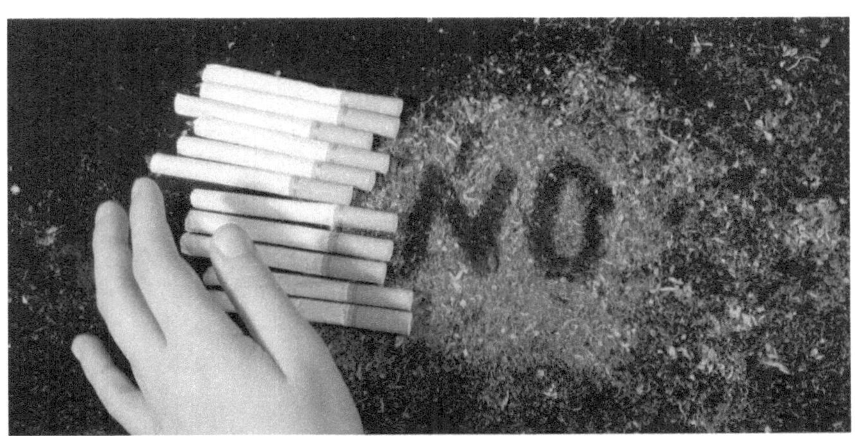

EXCESSIVE ALCOHOL CONSUMPTION

- Excessive alcohol use can lead to a range of health problems, including liver disease, heart disease, and addiction.
- If you choose to drink alcohol, do so in moderation (up to one drink per day for women and up to two drinks per day for men).
- Know your limits and seek help if you find it challenging to control your alcohol consumption.

UNHEALTHY EATING HABITS

- Overeating, binge eating, and consuming excessive junk food can lead to obesity, diabetes, and heart disease.
- Practice mindful eating, focus on balanced nutrition, and avoid emotional eating.
- Seek support from a registered dietitian or nutritionist for healthier eating habits.

SEDENTARY LIFESTYLE

- Prolonged sitting and lack of physical activity contribute to numerous health issues, including obesity and cardiovascular disease.
- Incorporate regular physical activity into your daily routine. Find activities you enjoy to make exercise a habit.

POOR SLEEP HABITS

- Inadequate sleep can lead to a host of health problems, including fatigue, mood disturbances, and increased risk of chronic diseases.
- Prioritize good sleep hygiene and aim for 7-9 hours of quality sleep per night.

STRESS AND COPING MECHANISMS

- Engaging in harmful coping mechanisms, such as excessive stress eating or substance abuse, can worsen stress-related health issues.
- Learn healthy stress management techniques, such as meditation, exercise, and seeking support from a therapist or counselor.

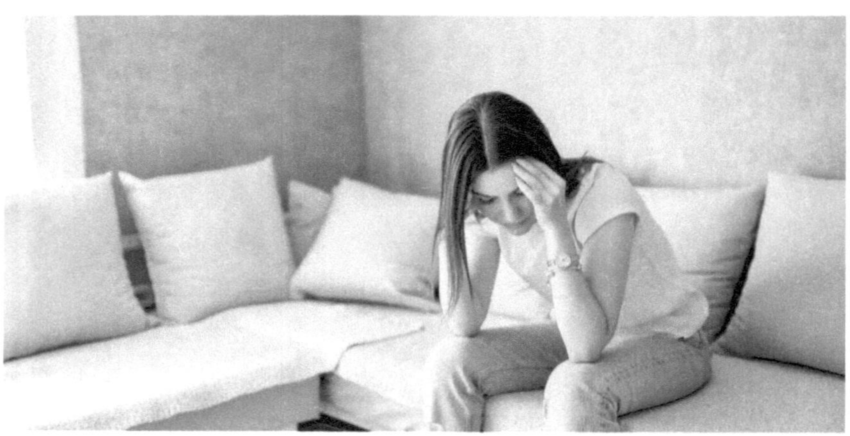

- Engaging in unprotected sex or risky sexual behavior can lead to sexually transmitted infections (STIs) and unwanted pregnancies.
- Use protection and practice safe sex. Get regular STI screenings if sexually active.

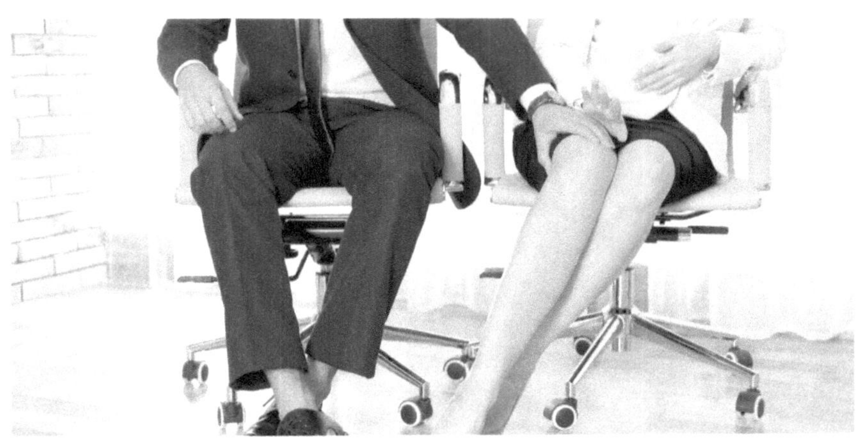

SUBSTANCE ABUSE

- Misuse of prescription drugs, recreational drugs, or other substances can have severe health consequences.
- Seek help from healthcare professionals or addiction specialists if you struggle with substance abuse issues.

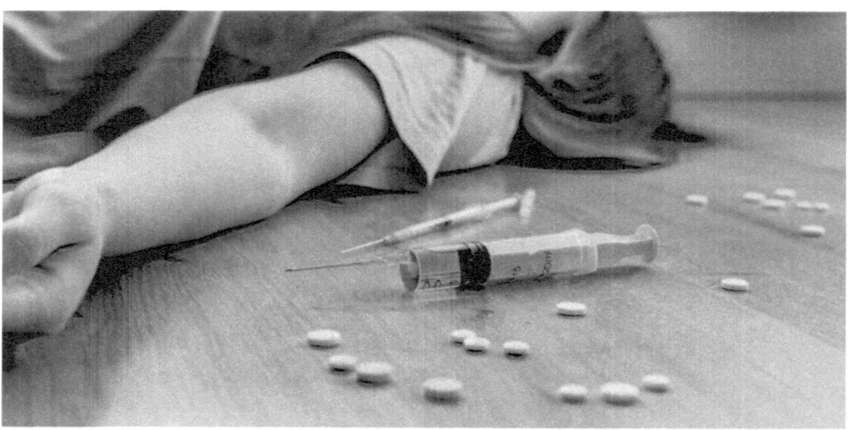

NEGLECTING MENTAL HEALTH

- Ignoring mental health needs can lead to chronic stress, anxiety, depression, and other mental health disorders.
- Prioritize your mental well-being by seeking therapy or counseling when needed and practicing self-care.

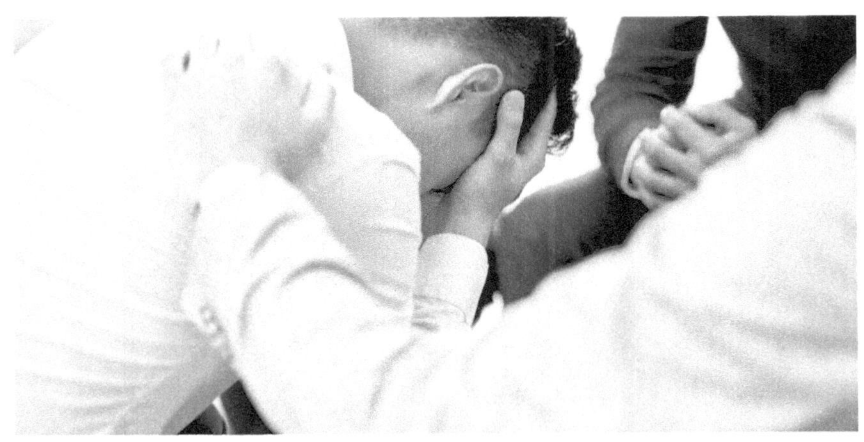

RECKLESS DRIVING AND RISKY BEHAVIOR

- Engaging in risky driving behaviors, like speeding or driving under the influence, can result in accidents and injury.
- Always obey traffic laws and never drive while impaired.

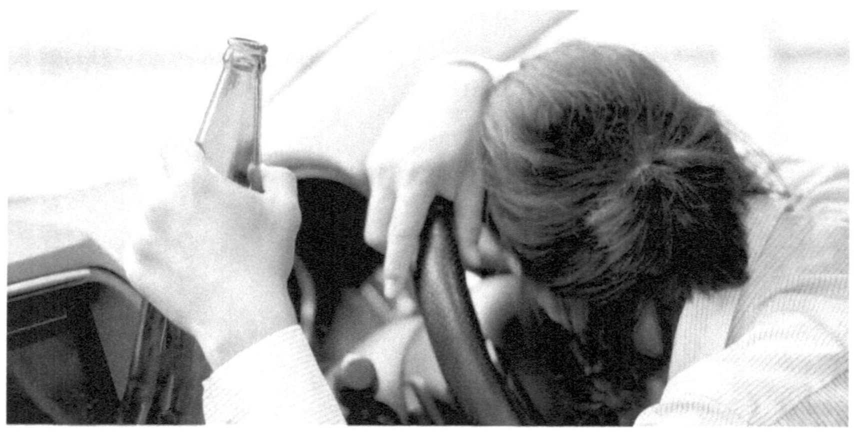

HYGIENE
AND
SANITATION

Personal Hygiene

Handwashing

Wash your hands frequently with soap and water for at least 20 seconds, especially before eating, after using the restroom, and after being in public places. Handwashing helps prevent the spread of germs.

Oral Hygiene

Brush your teeth at least twice a day and floss daily to maintain good dental hygiene. Regular dental check-ups are also important.

Personal Hygiene

Bathing

Take regular showers or baths to keep your skin clean and reduce the risk of skin infections.

Hair Care

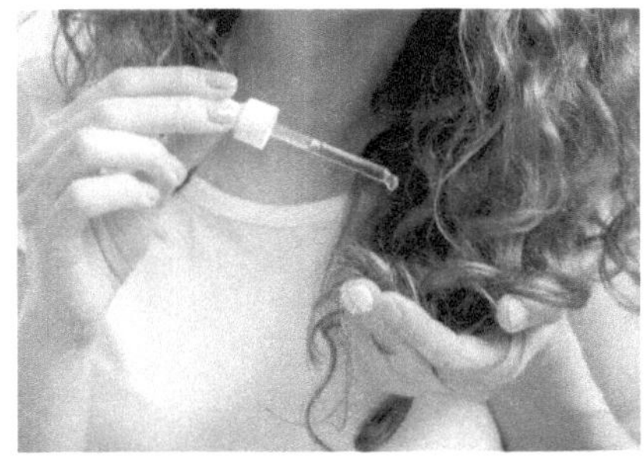

Keep your hair clean by washing it regularly and maintaining good scalp hygiene.

Nail Care

Trim your nails regularly and keep them clean to prevent the buildup of dirt and bacteria.

Personal Hygiene

Clothing

Change into clean clothes regularly and wash them as needed. Properly launder and store your clothing to prevent mold and bacteria growth.

Foot Care

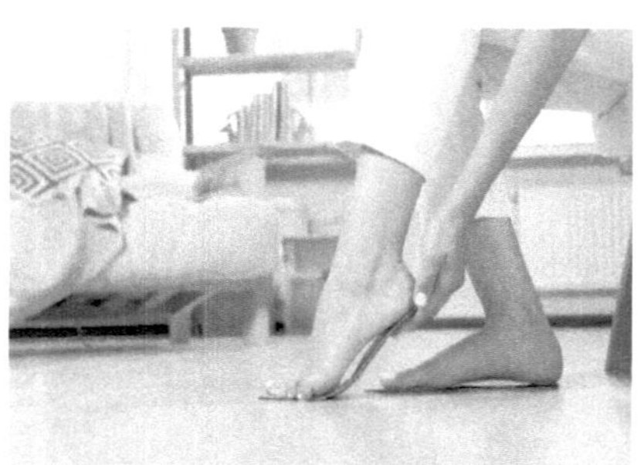

Keep your feet clean and dry to prevent fungal infections. Wear clean socks and well-fitting shoes.

Personal Hygiene

Clothing

Change into clean clothes regularly and wash them as needed. Properly launder and store your clothing to prevent mold and bacteria growth.

Foot Care

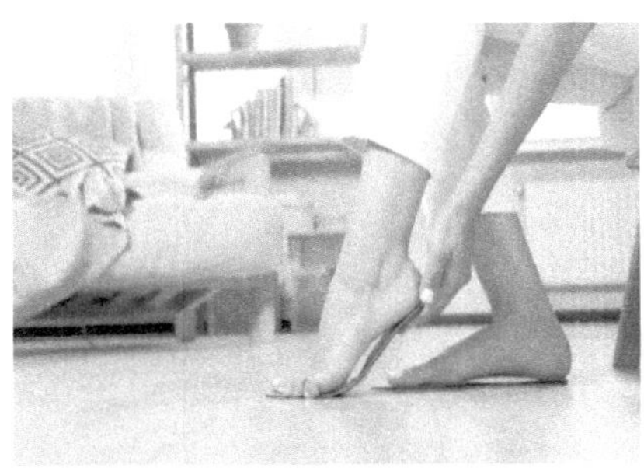

Keep your feet clean and dry to prevent fungal infections. Wear clean socks and well-fitting shoes.

FOOD AND WATER SAFETY

Food Handling

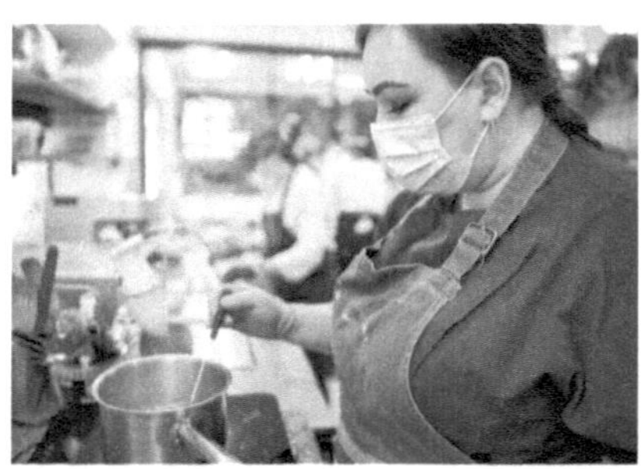

Practice safe food handling by washing your hands before preparing or eating food, cooking food thoroughly, and refrigerating perishable items promptly.

Water Quality

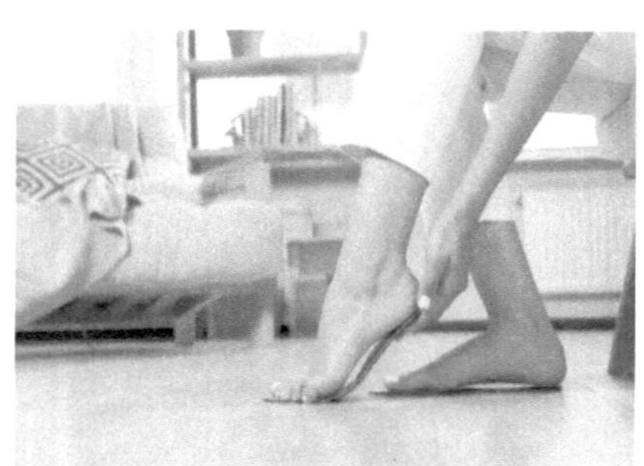

Ensure that the water you consume is clean and safe. If necessary, use water purification methods such as boiling, filtering, or using water purification tablets.

HOUSEHOLD HYGIENE

Cleaning

Regularly clean and disinfect frequently touched surfaces, such as doorknobs, countertops, and light switches. Use appropriate cleaning products and follow instructions.

Waste Disposal

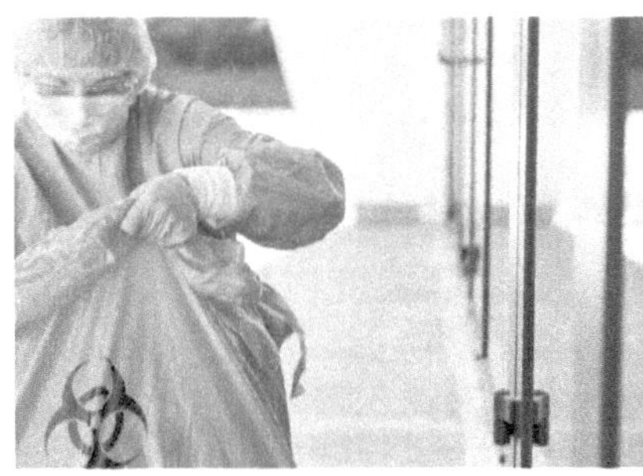

Dispose of waste, including trash and recyclables, properly in designated containers. Follow local guidelines for waste disposal.

Toilet Hygiene

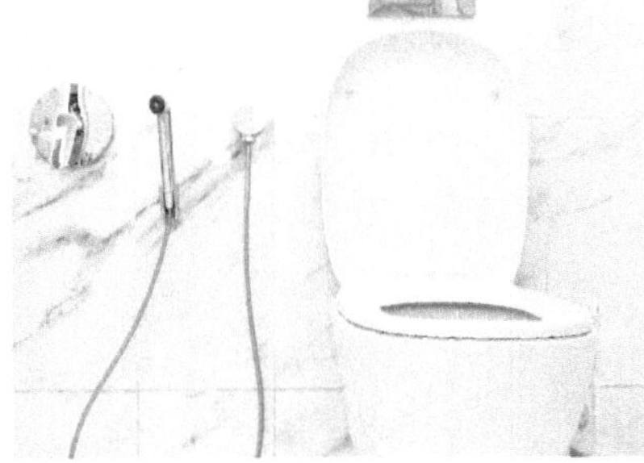

Maintain proper toilet hygiene by flushing waste and using toilet paper or bidets for cleaning. Wash your hands thoroughly after using the restroom.

COMMUNITY SANITATION

Sewage and Drainage

Ensure that sewage is disposed of safely and that drainage systems are functioning properly to prevent contamination of water sources.

Public Toilets

Use public restrooms and toilets responsibly, following proper hygiene practices to keep them clean and safe for others.

Vector Control

Take measures to control disease-carrying vectors, such as mosquitoes, by eliminating breeding sites and using protective measures like insect repellent and bed nets.

PERSONAL PROTECTIVE EQUIPMENT (PPE)

Face Masks

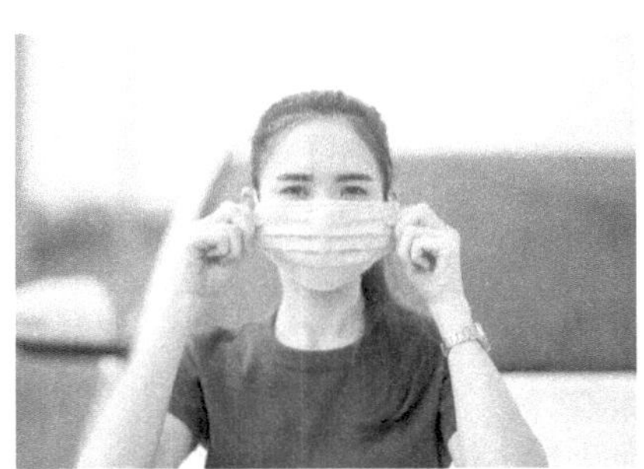

During contagious disease outbreaks, wearing face masks can help reduce the spread of respiratory droplets and protect both the wearer and others.

Gloves

Use disposable gloves when cleaning, handling waste, or providing care to someone who is ill. Dispose of gloves properly after use.

GENETIC PREDISPOSITION

INHERITED TRAITS

Genetic predisposition results from specific variations or mutations in an individual's genes. These genetic variations can be passed down from one generation to the next.

MULTIFACTORIAL

Most health conditions are influenced by a combination of genetic, environmental, and lifestyle factors. Genetic predisposition is just one piece of the puzzle.

COMMON EXAMPLES

- Cancer: Certain genetic mutations, such as BRCA1 and BRCA2 for breast and ovarian cancer, can increase the risk of developing these diseases.
- Cardiovascular Diseases: Genetic factors can contribute to conditions like heart disease, hypertension, and high cholesterol levels.
- Autoimmune Diseases: Conditions like rheumatoid arthritis, type 1 diabetes, and lupus can have a genetic component.
- Neurological Disorders: Genetic factors play a role in conditions like Alzheimer's disease, Parkinson's disease, and multiple sclerosis.
- Mental Health Disorders: Genetic predisposition can increase the likelihood of developing mental health conditions like depression, bipolar disorder, and schizophrenia.

PREVENTIVE MEASURES

People with a genetic predisposition to certain conditions can often take preventive measures to reduce their risk. This may include lifestyle modifications, regular screenings, and early intervention.

COMMUNITY AND SOCIAL CONNECTIONS

MENTAL AND EMOTIONAL SUPPORT

Social connections provide emotional support, helping individuals cope with stress, anxiety, and life's challenges. Strong social networks can reduce the risk of depression and loneliness.

PHYSICAL HEALTH

Research suggests that people with strong social connections tend to have better physical health. Social interactions can boost the immune system, lower blood pressure, and improve overall well-being.

SENSE OF BELONGING

Being part of a community and having social connections gives individuals a sense of belonging, which can contribute to a positive self-identity and self-esteem.

REDUCED ISOLATION

Social connections reduce feelings of isolation and can provide companionship, particularly for those who live alone or are going through major life changes.

ENVIRONMENTAL FACTORS

AIR QUALITY

- Clean air is essential for respiratory health. Poor air quality, polluted with pollutants, allergens, and particulate matter, can lead to respiratory diseases, allergies, and other health issues.
- To improve air quality indoors, ensure proper ventilation and consider using air purifiers.

WATER QUALITY

- Access to clean and safe drinking water is crucial for overall health. Contaminated water can lead to waterborne diseases and other health problems.
- Ensure that your drinking water source is regularly tested and treated if necessary.

GREEN SPACES AND NATURE

- Access to parks, green spaces, and natural environments can have a positive impact on mental and physical health. Spending time in nature reduces stress, anxiety, and depression and promotes physical activity.
- Make an effort to spend time in natural settings and incorporate outdoor activities into your routine.

HEALTHY FOOD ENVIRONMENTS

- Access to fresh, healthy, and affordable food is vital for maintaining a balanced diet and preventing diet-related diseases like obesity and diabetes.
- Support local farmers' markets and initiatives that promote access to fresh produce and healthier food options in your community.

SAFE HOUSING AND SHELTER

- Safe and stable housing conditions are essential for overall well-being. Inadequate housing can lead to health problems, including respiratory issues and mental stress.
- Advocate for safe and affordable housing policies and support organizations that provide shelter and housing assistance to those in need.

NOISE POLLUTION

- High levels of noise pollution can lead to stress, sleep disturbances, and even hearing loss. Reducing noise pollution in your environment can improve your quality of life.
- Use noise-cancelling headphones or earplugs when needed, and advocate for noise reduction policies in your community.

WASTE MANAGEMENT

- Proper waste disposal and recycling practices are essential for preventing environmental contamination and public health hazards.
- Follow waste disposal guidelines in your area and support recycling and waste reduction efforts.

CLIMATE AND WEATHER PATTERNS

- Climate conditions can affect health through extreme weather events, heatwaves, and the spread of vector-borne diseases.
- Stay informed about climate-related risks and take appropriate precautions to protect your health during extreme weather events.

ENVIRONMENTAL FACTORS